Just

Rewind

By M.A.R.K.S.

To my family, friends, and last but not least, my enemies.

Thanks.

Hopefully not based on a true story....

Prologue

If you thought this book was one of the types of books that are listed below, close the book and give it to your local thrift store (You know, the one on Main Street. You stopped going there last year.) This is not a biography, if you don't count biographies of fictional characters. This isn't exactly a murder, if you don't count that one guy on the news who was killed in Chapter 1 (oops, spoiler), or the ending, which has a possibility of death.

This definitely isn't a fantasy with flying sparkly unicorns or fierce dragons who breathe in oxygen and exhale lit-up methane or helium or any other flammable gas (it's scientifically impossible; therefore, it's a fantasy).

But this is a sciency, realistic, fantasy-like fiction story that all starts on a very normal Tuesday in the city of Denver, Colorado. (It has some logic to it.)

WARNING!!!

Don't eat or drink anything while reading this.

If you do, you'll regret it.

CHAPTER 1

The TV was loud and on the news channel with a reporter at a crime scene. "Harry Humble was killed by David Boise for being too humble. Now Mr. Boise has been arrested, and he shall be charged for…" I turned the TV off and got off the couch.

"Mom. I'm going to my lab to work on one of my inventions!!" I shouted, halfway across the house. My mother yelled back to me,

"Are you going to do something stupid like make a potassium bomb out of bananas and blow up your lab? It cost us fifty thousand dollars to fix up the place! Don't you remember? We could have gone broke!! At least you made that 'lead to gold' machine to get us some quick money for your damage, but the machine broke down and you lost the design, so we only got forty thousand dollars' worth of gold. I never thought your college funds would come in handy, but they did. It paid off the remaining $10,000. Don't worry, you'll get a fully covered scholarship and go to university for free!"

I sighed and told my mom, "No, nothing will explode in this project," and I turned and said, "Hopefully," under my breath.

"I heard that!" My mom yelled.

"My brain will explode because of thinking too much." I told her.

"If you want to work on it, build a shed in the yard and work on it there. I'll give you 500 dollars, and you should go straight to the hardware store and get whatever you need to build it."

I needed a break. I turned around and turned on the television again. I felt that my mother did not want to cause any trouble, but she did not want to interfere with my inventions. The news was reporting about a person who found 45 million dollars in diamonds buried underground in his backyard.

One of the past owners of the house was a millionaire who died in the 1960s. They then showed the house. I dropped the remote. I yelled to call my mom and my siblings, and right there was the house we used to live in. "45 million right out in the backyard, and you guys never even dug it up and found it!" My mom angrily said. I didn't know what to do; I paced around the house and around the yard and thought and thought and thought and thought (you probably see where this is going.)

A FEW HOURS LATER...

I asked my mom for around 500 more dollars. She gave it to me after asking me what I was going to do with it, and I told her that I was going to make a lot of money with it. My mother always trusted me. I would never let her down.

CHAPTER 2

I went to the relatively new store, and I walked down the aisles of the store, slowly picking out everything I needed. After walking through around 30 of the aisles, I got some batteries, certain chemicals, and a big foldable metal crate. I went up to the blond-haired, 16-year-old cashier, and he looked at me with a curious and surprised face. "That'll be nine hundred sixty-seven dollars and forty-two cents, without tax. Would you like a 10% student discount?" He said, putting the small items in bags and skipping the large ones.

 "Yeah sure, why not!" I said happily.

"Okay, so that will be nine hundred forty-seven dollars and thirty-eight cents." He said. "And what are you going to do with it?" He asked.

"It's for a project," I told him.

"And are you going to tip me?" The cashier asked.

"Sure!" I said, with a fun plan in my mind.

"What percentage of your purchase would you like to tip?" He asked.

"I'll put in the number," I told him.

"Okay!" He chirped cheerfully. (Don't try this at home, kids, or at the store. I'm warning you! It will not work in real life. It's a story.)

"Actually, I can't find the negative sign. Can you type it in the system? -100%." I told him, hoping he forgot basic elementary school math. He typed it in.

"Thank you! That'll be going straight into my account! I'm gonna check my bank account balance right now!" He said, unprofessionally. I walked out of the shop with the "paid by the employee" things.

I took the things home and went to the shed that was in the yard that my mom told me to put my inventions in and started building. I worked day and night for a few days until it was complete. I sketched out the (complicated) way the machine worked and I knew it would work, somehow. It was a time machine.

The way I learned to make a time machine was when I read a book on how to make it. It was titled: *An Idiot's Guide to Build a Time Machine, By F.R. Audlent.*
Nobody reads books nowadays; the information you can get from them is surprising.
I needed to test it; I needed to test my invention.

Today will be the best day of my life if this works out. It might fail, but it is good if I test it out first. I was outside; the light blue sky with no clouds in it let the sun's rays hit my skin.

I wanted to test it with an apple (yes, just a normal Red Delicious apple). I walked up to my time machine and put the Red Delicious apple in the time machine and set it to come in 10 seconds in the future. I set it to launch in 5 seconds, so I quickly stepped out of the machine and let the time machine transport the apple.

You see, when and where you send the apple is very important. For example, if you make it fall right on top of Isaac Newton's head from 1,000 feet in the air BEFORE he finds out about gravity then he would get knocked out, or he may even die. Gravity would only have been discovered decades or even centuries later.

If you dropped the apple 1,000 feet from the air onto the Wright brothers' first flight and made the plane crash, then there would have been a severe injury to one of those two, and the airplane would not have been invented in 1903. I could go on with many examples like this.

The apple came back, and it was in my shed. Success. This time, I will also remotely control it and send it back to 1563. So I sent it.
It fell on a farm and came back. The way I know this is because it smelled (and tasted) like cow dung.

After that I needed to do a human test. I was going to find my friend T.A., who I never considered a friend, and he never considered me as a friend, but rather an asset at most. You may find this weird, but you'll find out why soon. I put on some slippers and was about to open the door to go find him, but right then I heard the signature knock that was made in a certain tune that I cannot explain in words.

I knew who it was, and I knew he could read my mind. Ever wondered who I meant by T.A.? The Author.

CHAPTER 3

I opened the door.

"Come in, come in, and you write the books, so why exactly are you in one?" I asked The Author. He came inside and sat on the couch, ignoring my question. My mom saw him, and her eyes grew big with fear and excitement.

"Are you here to make our story exciting AND am I going to be alive when the book is done? Usually the mom dies in most stories, right?" My mother asked.

"No, no. I've come to complain about your son, and yes, hopefully you'll be alive," The Author said, stressing the word "hopefully" a bit too much. Now it was my turn to feel scared and excited. "Tell me what you need to tell me, and don't keep the reader waiting."

I told The Author and after I said that, his face turned into a scowl, and in two seconds, he was calm, and he said, "I can keep the reader waiting as long as I want." He said, but quickly added, "But now is a good time to inform you, and the readers, what I came here for. First of all, DON'T CALL ME T.A.!" He yelled. "What should we call you?" I asked politely.

"By the name on the cover of the book or the one on the copyright page, whichever is longer, thank you very much. If it's not there, do some research and find out what it is." He told me politely.
"No, it is way too hard," I said.

The Author was furious. "YOU IDIOT, YOU CANNOT EVEN SAY YOUR AUTHOR'S NAME! JUST FIND IT AND READ IT!!!"

"I'll try on my own time, thank you very much," I said.

"Second, you did not tell the reader about the butterfly effect, you know, the effect where a tiny thing indirectly causes a huge thing to occur." he said curtly.

"I did explain about it, with the apple and all that," I said, annoyed by him. He then said, "It was in your script to say the words 'butterfly effect' in your explanation! Why didn't you!" He said, somewhat angry, upset, and disappointed.

"We are in a book! We don't have scripts! Plus, you write everything!!" I argued. "Hmm..." He made a noncommittal noise under his breath. "True, I totally agree," he said cheerfully.

His face changed from happy to angry in one second and he said, "The third thing is... why did you make a time machine!"

CHAPTER 4

"Well, it's because authors like you never pay us characters a single penny in books like these when we really need it, and even if y'all do, you take it away at the end of the story! I'm going to try to get the money myself!" I argued.

"Well, I can do anything with a pen and a book, see!" He started writing something. "I can make you do anything I want!" He said it and I began to sing a lullaby *to myself*! "Rock-a-bye baby on the treetop...."

I fell asleep in a couple seconds and woke up on my bed in what felt like a second. The Author was a few feet away from me. "See what I mean? I have a pen that can control you due to me being the author of this story. I control you." He spoke.

"A time machine isn't the solution for everything. Sometimes, you can just ask!" he kindly said.

"Who will I go to for millions of dollars and stuff that I cannot get in the present!" I said, thinking he was a total idiot. "Me, of course!" He added, "Eventually, when I have the money," under his breath. "But of course this story is a time travel story, and it won't be a time travel story without time travel, so you've got to time travel in the time traveling story! Did I say 'time traveling' too much?" He said, redundantly.

I then said, "Yeah, you did." Right then my mom burst into the room. "Stop bothering my son!" She said, and right then The Author broke into a crooked smile and sarcastically said, "Your son, his son, her son, their son, and arson are all pretty much the same thing, right?"

I don't know how, but the words just flew out of my mouth, like it was predetermined, only it was. I guess The Author just used the pen and made me say it. "Arson is the crime of putting someone's property on fire or blowing it up intentionally. Of course, you will most likely be punished for blowing anything up in most cases."

I smiled, proud to explain something I knew absolutely nothing about. The Author was furious and took a step toward me.

"Why are you taking credit for what I did? For what I put in your mind! I will have revenge, and trust me, you will regret it..." He then vanished into thin air, with no trace of him being there a second ago.

Chapter 5

He came back a few seconds after "Totally kidding, but I still need to go. Anyway, if anyone comes to take you, you're protected by intellectual property! Also get money using the time machine if you want to, but make sure the story ends well. Also, don't go back to your property to take the 45 million. You are not allowed to do that..." He then vanished peacefully after that.

I thought about a way to make money easily. I got nothing. Nothing. I went to my actual friend's house. His name is Richard, and he has a lot of ideas for everything.

His dad works in a big fast-food company behind the scenes as a manager. He even knows the CEO of the company.

Richard's mom is missing and presumed dead because she got kidnapped and probably killed. It happened 2 years ago. I knocked on the door. "Hey, Denver! Come on in!" After he let me come in, I went in.

"What if I told you I made a time machine," I said after sitting on the couch, then he laughed and said, "Well I'd think you're an idiot who probably came here to joke around and eat chips. If you came here for chips, then I'll give you some."

He went into the kitchen. I yelled to him, "No thanks! Just come over to my place!"

"Okay, if you say so!" We then walked out the door and trotted over to my place.

"Look at my new shed! I built it! My mom told me to build it because I blew up my bedroom once while making an invention." I exclaimed.

"Wow, that is cool. Where is the 'time machine' you said you made?" He said, adding air quotes to the words "time machine."

"Here my friend, is the time machine," I said to him.

I opened the shed door and Richard's mouth dropped open in awe. "What the..." He was speechless. He finally turned to me and asked, "Have you tested it yet?"

I then told him clearly, "I have tested it with apples but not with humans yet. If you want, you can test it for me, and if you die, I'll send a robot to this second and place a note inside it saying to not send you and make certain adjustments." He was satisfied with my answer.

"Okay where do you want to go?" I asked.

"Maybe 1 hour from the present time?"

"Sure, I'll set it up, and do not touch any of the buttons!"

I then set the time machine up to send him 1 hour later. He climbed in. I closed the time machine's silver door, covering Richard and the hundred buttons on the control panel of the machine.

I watched as the time machine buzzed and disappeared. I waited. Waited. I waited for what seemed like a year. I checked my watch and there was 2 minutes left until the scheduled arrival of Richard.

2 minutes later...

All of a sudden, I heard the buzz of the machine. It had come back. I walked up to it. "Richard, are you okay?"

I opened the door. "BOO!" Richard said, jumping on me. We both laughed hysterically. Then he said "It was fine, but it was unlike any experience I have ever had in my entire life. Just to be sure, what is the time and day now?"

I checked my watch "Tuesday, 5:32 PM, June 25. So now who's the one that comes over to eat chips, huh?" I said, happily.

His face lit up and was sad at the same time, "If you can bring my mom back alive with your machine, I'll ask my dad to give you something! And also, I want to see my mother one last time, that is, if we can't bring her back. Can I come with you? Please? Won't you do it for your best friend? I'm practically begging you!"

He begged me.

"Of course! But I need to tell my mom and your father the procedures if we die or get lost in time. So, let's get started!"

Chapter 6

I told my mom and Richard's dad about the

procedures. Richard's dad thought I was an insane

idiot, and my mom said to do what's right and save

Richard's mom. Richard and I studied some parts

of the case, and I made him remember every detail

and where he saw his mom last.

   "At home, around 2:40 PM, Thursday, February 5,

2 years ago." He replied, excited to see his mom

again.

   "Do you have a picture of her? I forget what she

looks like. It has been 2 years you know," Richard

was prepared. He held out a picture of his mom

and I took, like 10 copies of it.

   My mom wished me good luck. Richard's dad

was still not convinced. I took some stuff, like my

homemade dart gun, so I can knock out anyone who came in our way. Some newspapers from the days Richard's mom was missing, so we can confront her with the facts. A knife, just in case. I took money, some old ID's, and finally, 2 old bus passes that were valid in that time period, for transportation.

In case you wanted to see it, here's the newspaper article:

"A 32-year-old woman named Sally James was reported missing yesterday. She was believed to be kidnapped and killed. She has an 11-year-old son named Richard James and a husband, Ronald James. Any sightings should be reported to the DPD and please email us or call the following number, 445-NEWS. Thanks!"

The time machine was portable, so I could carry it around.

We were ready. We climbed in. I pushed in the date quickly without a second thought.

The time traveling part was odd. The next chapter is how I felt and what I thought.

Chapter 7

Chapter 8

Blank.

I felt dead for a few seconds.

No emotions, no thoughts, nothing, just felt dead and blank. We arrived.

"I remember this like it was yesterday," Richard said, smiling.

"Um, Richard, that's because it is yesterday. I think I put in the wrong date! I'll fix it." I fixed it and we went back in time, again, feeling blank.
(I'm not gonna waste another chapter this time.)

We got off on the correct date on our second try. It felt like the present, probably because nothing changed much in our neighborhood.

"So, let's go find your mother!" I exclaimed. The time was exactly 10 AM.

"We should go to the electronics store first, to buy a location tracking device, it'll be very useful in the future." I told Richard.

"Okay," he said, bravely. We got a cab. We trotted into the store, grabbed a location tracking device, and paid for it (you were expecting me to steal it, weren't you?)

We walked out. "Now what?" Richard asked. "We should talk to your mother, and we should kidnap her, with her consent, of course." We took a taxi, and we went to Richard's house. During the ride, Richard and I had a quick chat about my hygiene. "Denver, no offense, but you smell bad."

"That's because I don't wear deodorant."

"Why don't you?"

"I'm nothing but paper and ink, so I don't sweat, and therefore, I don't stink."

"Then what is that smell?"

"I honestly have no clue, but it is definitely not me."

"You don't smell bad on the outside of the book, but on the inside of the book, you smell horrible."

I couldn't agree to this, no matter how true it may have been, and that the thought never came.

"So what you're saying is that I stink on the inside, right."

"Right."

"You also stink on the inside, Richard. In fact, almost everyone stinks on the inside. A quick test to see if they stink on the inside is asking the 3-word question: What is life? If they can respond to that, their inside is clean."

"What if they eat healthy?"

"Where did you get that from?"

"Well, if their inside is clean, they probably eat healthy right? Or else they would be suffering from diseases, and their inside wouldn't be clean."

"I was talking about their minds and souls, not their physical bodies! The worst of people could potentially be the cleanest physically."

"You're confusing."

I had steered the conversation away from the fact that I stank, mission accomplished.
We arrived at the house.

We knocked on the door "Richard, quick! HIDE!"
An 11-year-old Richard opened the door.
"Hello Denver, you look tall and old. Another experiment gone wrong, hasn't it?"
"Yeah. Growth potion."
"Well, what did you come here for?"
"To talk to your mother."
"Why?"
"Oh, I needed to tell her something," I said.
"Well, she's upstairs."

He gladly let me in. I found Richard's mother doing a sudoku, calm, unlike anything was ever going to happen in the next few hours, which was proof she knew nothing.

I shut the door. She noticed me. "Hello!" she said, cheerfully.

Then her face changed slightly when she noticed I was taller and seemed older and thought I probably had an experiment mishap (I was still learning how to make great inventions back then.)

"Another mishap?" She asked, concerned. I did not know where to begin. I carefully tossed one of the newspapers to her. She was shocked a bit once she read it, but then went to her normal face.

"This is a big prank, right? Wait. I'm gonna tell your mother." She said, angry.

"Mrs. James," I croaked. "You're dead." I said, quickly realizing that was a bad choice of words.

"Who me? I'm not calling your mother. I am calling the police." She said, reaching for her phone. "No, I mean..." I took a deep breath. "I made a time machine, and you go missing in the future and Richard and I wanted to save you so here we are. Come outside and I'll show you the older version of Richard. But here, see these newspapers." She looked at them shocked.

"Come on. Let's go see your son!" I said. I took her outside. Once Richard saw his mom he gulped and said: "Mom." He almost started crying but caught himself. He hugged his mom.

"Well, we came to smuggle you into the future. We need to kidnap you so your real kidnapper won't kidnap you." I told her. "At 2:40 we will smuggle you. Okay? I can't do it now because the newspaper said that you will get kidnapped at 2:40."

She wasn't convinced.
"Nothing bad will happen, I can assure you." I said.

"Really?"

"Really" Both Richard and I said, at the same time.

"Okay." She said.

Finally, it was 2:40, and I told her what to tell her son and husband, to prevent anything bad happening in the future.

"They think I'm going out to get some milk! That's sad! No wonder I'm in the headlines!" She said, her face sad and disgusted.

"How about this, do you want to get kidnapped?" I asked.

Chapter 9

"We could follow you and save you," I said.

"It may help us find your kidnappers!"

"What's in it for me?"

"Well, you may not have to worry about what's going to happen after we take you into the future. So, are you in?"

"No, just take me home."

   She went to talk with Richard. Right then The Author showed up behind me.

"So, what have you done so far?" He asked. "I saved Richard's mother! Well, almost." I said happily.

He said, "Well okay Mr. Colorado, I'm somewhat happy you did." I never even knew my last name was Colorado.

"Since when was my full name 'Denver Colorado?'"

"Since the start of the book. Hey, I'm terrible at coming up with names. City names are a great way to get names for y'all characters. If you want, you can file a name changing petition once you're 18 years old." He said.

"Fine. I accept my odd name. But you might as well have named me Chicago Illinois or Columbus Ohio or something cool!" I shouted. After hearing this he said, "Well I've got to go. See you soon. Don't let a time paradox happen!"

After she was gone, we set up the time machine. She said everything we told her to say to her husband and the 11-year-old Richard. We all went into the time machine.

I pushed in the buttons. "The time machine says it has a low battery. And we cannot leave the machine, or take it with us to the store, cause the battery will die in a few minutes, forever." I said, horrified.

I hate battery issues.

Chapter 10

"It said it could only go until 1 day before the launch date. Which means we'd have to live alongside our past selves!"

"We are so dead," Richard said, scared.

"We need another battery source. Anyone have batteries on them?"

"No," Richard and his mother said in unison.

"Well, you might as well go into the future alone, mom, you are considered missing." Richard said.

"No! It'll stop us from coming here and if we don't come here, we won't save her and send her into the future, but in the end, we won't be stopped by anyone. If we do that, it will be a time paradox! The Author said not to let that happen!" I said and continued, "This one guy had a theory: 'The grandfather paradox' which is where you go back in time, make your grandparent not give birth to your mom or dad, like preventing their marriage or killing them, and one of your parents won't be born, so you won't be born and you won't prevent your grandparent from being killed or prevent them from giving birth to your parent, so in the end what happened?"

"Confusing. Oh well, so long, dear idea of mine!" Richard said.

"Wait... I might have batteries in my tranquilizer dart gun." I took it out and removed the batteries.

"YAY!!" We all said at the same time.

I replaced the double A batteries, which is the worst thing to power a time machine with. ESPECIALLY the Few-Dollars-Only brand 4-for-1 dollar kind. Only lasted for like, 4 trips. Never trust cheap brands. Buy batteries from good brands and good stores, like Apartment Depot or Fall-Mart (not to be confused with Autumn-Mart), or Everything-in-our-store-is-slightly-cheaper-but-you-have-to-pay-a-membership-fee-to-buy-stuff-from-here-so-I-MIGHT-come-to-our-store-if-I-were-you-CO -You should really see that store's sign.

And the machine was good to go. We went back to the future and went straight to Richard's house. Richard's dad's jaw dropped. "Sally," he said in disbelief.
"I told you we'd get her back. Now we need a good story on what happened."

I said. "How about this, you got temporary amnesia because of a drug someone gave you and got kidnapped and kept in a cabin in the middle of a forest, and you were fed through the mail slot, and had a bathroom and whatnot, and one day the door broke down and you escaped and came here, to Denver, by pure coincidence. Nice story, eh?" I told them.

The story needed some tweaking to make it logical and the story was published and in the headlines. Here is the article that was published.

Dead woman found alive (with interview):
A 34-year-old Denverite woman named Sally James was reported missing around 2 years ago and was believed to be kidnapped and killed. But folks, somehow, by a total miracle, she came back to Denver and she says that she had temporary retrograde amnesia cause of a hard blow on the head while someone attacked her, and got maliciously kidnapped and kept in an underground bunker in the middle of a forest, and she was fed, but did not see the person feeding her, and had a bathroom and a couch, and one day the bulletproof door broke down (it was probably mass produced and made low quality in Chinese factories- I've got nothing against making things in bulk in Chinese factories, but when it's a bulletproof door, do a quality check!) After that, she left and saw her surroundings, and used the sun's

direction to come to Denver, by hiking through the forest and finding her way around. We did an interview with her.

Here is the phone interview:

"News Reporter: Hello Mrs. James, it seems you need no introduction, as the woman who survived in a bunker for years, you know, since you're in the headlines. So, tell us your story please!

Sally James: What should I tell you first?

NR: Well, who do you think kidnapped you?

SJ: I am honestly not sure.

NR: Well, do you think they knew you?

SJ: I think I was a randomly selected victim.

NR: Have you seen the kidnapper's face?

SJ: No, when they leave me food, they are usually completely covered, so much that I don't know the color of his or her skin, and I am not even sure if it's one person.

NR: Do you remember the kidnapping?

SJ: Well, I somewhat remember the iron hammer hitting my head, but I was knocked out for a while, and I got a concussion. I got amnesia to some level after that, but now I remember most of my memories. So no, I only remember being in the bunker unharmed, except for my head, of course, and yeah, I don't remember anything from the kidnapping.

NR: There are rumors that all this never happened. Is it true?"

CHAPTER 11

PART 2 OF INTERVIEW:

"SJ: A rumor is a rumor; it is usually not true.

NR: The police can't find any bunkers in the place you thought you can from. Are you sure you were in a bunker?

SJ: Yes, I was.

NR: And there was no camera footage!

SJ: Is that a statement?

NR: Yes.

SJ: What I said was the truth! If you have good questions email them. Goodbye.

NR: WAIT!!

(Sally hangs up.) "

Sally is clearly hiding something important. If you have any information, please let us know by email, or call us.

So, then we were done for. Exposed. Doomed.
Done for.

I have no more synonyms for doom and exposed
and done for.

I looked it up...

Revealed. Uncovered. Unveiled. Concluded.
Finished. Over.

I think you get my point.

Or maybe you don't.

I don't care.

I just didn't know what to do.

So... I went to Richard's house and talked to him.

"Richard! What do we do?!" I told him.

"We could tell everyone the truth!" Richard said.

"We'll be locked up or threatened if we tell the
truth! The time machine will be taken from us." I
yelled, taking a step back.

  I think I yelled that too loud, cause right then a
guy came knocking at the door. He had dirty blond

hair and seemed like a homeless man who was drunk.

"I found you, murderer. You killed my buddy two years ago! Luckily, I escaped, or else I may've been your victim. You look not a day older than the time I last saw you. I am going to call the police!" He said, eerily and reached for his pocket, probably for a phone, but there was nothing in it besides a tiny bag with a white powder in it, which fell out.

"Not if I do it first." I said, and grabbed the tiny packet and slammed the door. I grabbed a phone and called the police and told them there was a drunk (and possibly high) drug addict knocking from door to door. The cops came, examined, and identified the powder as a drug, and caught the man. The cops dragged him into the police vehicle.

"I will get you..." were his final words to me before he went into the vehicle.

"Hopefully we don't go into the federal witness protection program." I said, trying to make the situation feel more positive.

"Hey Denver, don't you think what the guy said was kind of strange?" Richard told me.
"Yeah, it is kind of strange, don't you think?" Richard's mother commented.
"He's probably a drunk idiot who doesn't know what he's talking about. But what he said was kind of eerie though." I said, shivering at the thought of the guy being right.

"Maybe we must go back in time for something and end up killing his friend, or at least, making him think his friend is dead and he saw us through an open window and came knocking. But who could the friend be?" Richard said.

"I mean, that would explain a lot. And no, I have no clue on who his friend would be." I said, surprised at the amount of intelligence my somewhat not smart friend had, (I'm simply not humble.)

I guess he's smarter than I realized, and I guess he's a smart kid after all, in his own ways.

The Author appeared right behind us and said, "You know, Richard's right, and you'll find out why soon..." He vanished.

We were all silent for like, 2 minutes until I broke the silence and said, "Well people, I feel like there's a bumpy ride ahead of us."

CHAPTER 12

I checked the news for updates on the addict.

I found 2 articles. Here is the most accurate article that was posted a day after the incident:

ARTICLE:

A man named Stuart Atkinson was caught with 5 milligrams of a certain drug yesterday and he claims that a 13-year-old kid named Denver killed his friend. The police have ignored this claim. Denver was the one to call the police on Stuart after he saw that a white powder fell out of his pocket. The man shall be sentenced to jail for 20 years because it has been found out that he also sells drugs. According to Denver, the drunk or possibly high man came knocking at his door. He saw the drug fall out of his pocket and called the police.

And yeah, I guess I'm on the news. I feel like the guy was telling the truth to some extent. Maybe we *do* go back in time and do something to his friend. Hopefully not.

I was at Richard's house. We were in the middle of a conversation between me, Richard, and his mother. But right then I heard a knock at the door. I went toward the door, opened it, and right there were like, 20 news reporters and they all had microphones and cameras. The one at the door said, "Well kid, where's Sally James?"

CHAPTER 13

"She's not at home!" I lied.

"Then who is that over there?" A reporter said, pointing at Richard's mom.
"You are on private property, and I am ordering you to leave or else I'll call the police."

The mob dispersed and started recording us from the streets, but I closed the door, covered up all the windows, and called the police. The dispatcher said they'll take care of it. They were shooed away like flies. So, after the tough day I went back home and jumped in bed, my eyes staring at the white ceiling, and my brain processing everything that happened that day. Once my brain was done processing everything, I thought about the solution to my problem. I thought about it for a while. And I got the solution. But I forgot it. And I got the solution again. But I forgot it. And I got the solution *again*. But I forgot it. This time I actually forgot it.

Except I got the idea back in my head, but this time I actually had the idea. It was a great idea. I was going to go back in time again. (I am not going to elaborate now about it.)

I slept for a bit, and I had a lucid dream (those dreams where you control what you do.) It was about me flying around the city and time traveling, which are two things that do not go together. So, after that, I woke up at around 2:00 a.m. and found out that I had been asleep for 4 hours. I slept again and woke up again at around 8:00 a.m. and called Richard to my house through my phone.

"What did you call me for?" asked Richard.

"Do you want to go back in time again?" I asked him back.

"Nah, not after what happened with the news reporters." He told me.

"We can change that!" I said to him, with a wide grin on my face, which he did not see due to him being around half a mile away.

"We can?" He asked.

"What are time machines for? Of course we can change the past! We just need to know what to do in the past!" I told him happily.

 "I'll be right there." He said. After a few minutes, I heard the doorbell ring and rushed downstairs and opened the door and I let Richard come inside.

  "How do you think we can change all this?" Richard asked me, once we got to my room, (although I'd really prefer to call it a LABORATORY!)

  "I think we should go back in time and change everything, but not affect the future too much," I told him.

  So, after that I thought with him, spitting out every solution we could think of, most of them being terrible ideas. And I finally came up with a very good idea and I told my idea to Richard, my brain spilling every detail of the idea to him.

"Okay, so you're saying that we go back in time, make a bunker in the middle of a forest, put my mom in it, come every week and give her food, and tell her to come home after 2 years? That's a crazy idea. How do you expect us to pull it off?" He asked.

"Trust me Richie, I know what I'm doing."

CHAPTER 14

"You haven't called me Richie in this whole book! Why'd you use the nickname now?" He asked.

"It was to build up action for the end of the chapter. A good story needs suspense and drama," I told him.

"Okay, so how do we execute the plan?" He asked me.

"We could just follow it step by step," I said.

"Hey Denver, your time machine can 'teleport' to another place at the same time, right? You could just set the time as the present and set the place to a different place." Richard told me.

"Yep." I told him.

"So, we could go to the hardware store, buy everything we need and teleport to the building site, which I'd assume is in the middle of the forest, and pretend we didn't do anything!"

"I never knew you had a brain, Richard! Good thinking!" I said. He looked offended. "I was kidding," I lied.

So, then I made plans for a bunker in the middle of the forest. It took a while, but I knew I could do it.

I'd assume the readers have questions.

How would Richard's mom get water?

We'd drill a well; I made an invention a few months ago that makes wells very easily, and I also took an online course on plumbing a while ago, so I think we're good.

What about the bathroom?

I'd install a septic tank.

And electricity?

Everything would be powered by 2 big rechargeable batteries and me and Richard would charge them at Richard's house when one of them would be in use in the bunker.

How big would it be?

15 feet by 15 feet

And for the money?

We'll make Richard's mom make things. She could knit sweaters or sew clothes or make art, and so on, and we'd sell them.
The land?

We'd go back to the 1980's and buy it cheaply.

For any other questions, you'd have to think.

Chapter 15

So we took a loan at the bank for $7,000. The practicalities of that shall not be discussed, as this is a story, and anything can happen. I was done making the designs for the bunker in the middle of the forest. Seems a bit far-fetched, right? Of course it is.

 So we got ready to go back in time and build the bunker.

   Again, we stepped into the time machine and I pushed in the buttons, and we were all set.

"Are all of you ready?" I asked everyone.
"Yes, we are all ready," Richard and his mom said.

And then we were off 2 years into the past, feeling dead during the journey. The blank feeling, with no emotions felt... blank. I actually never thought this plan would work and I still don't think this will but it's still worth a try anyway.

I set the location to the hardware store so that we could start buying stuff immediately.

So we went into the store and picked out the things we needed.

So what did we need? Well, we needed a lot of things. First, the bunker would need a steel frame. So I picked out some steel rods. We also needed some wood, a floor, running water, and so on. So I got all those things and for the water I got anything necessary for the plumbing. Some comfy stuff was also needed: chairs, a mini kitchen, to heat stuff up and to wash her hands and make stuff, books (to read, of course, if you thought it was to eat, well... I have one word for you: get out. Okay, that was two words, but still,) and a lot more things.

  And the septic tank was bought online, due to it not being available at the store. The location was set to a house that nobody lives at, it's like how scammers make people send money to locations where nobody lives at, and make people pick up the money from there. The home was actually my uncle's new home, which he just bought a while ago, and it was on the market for over 4 years, due to it needing major renovation, and its price being way too high. My uncle did not care at all. He bought it and renovated it, and now it seems like a great home to live in. I've only been there twice before, because he just bought the home, like 2 months ago. I don't really know him too well. Well, enough about my maternal uncle.

Time to start our mission.

Chapter 16

I went into the forest with the things, which were transported with the time machine's "teleportation" feature. It was complicated. Moving things around, constantly buying a ton of stuff. People look at us a bit weirdly, as if a child could not be rich. But then again, is it not strange for two tweens to buy construction supplies from a hardware store, happily dragging a ton of stuff from the store along with them?

But most importantly, I felt like I was constantly being watched by someone. Intuition is great; your intuition may warn you at times, and it may mess with you at times. But usually, it is correct. Correct, I think it shall be this time. Correct. Hopefully, it is not. But won't the story be more exciting with a person watching us, and finally we confront them?

It will, but I won't risk my neck for the pleasure of some person I don't know. You, reader, are that person. I think there is a person watching me, that isn't you.

I have a weird feeling that I am being constantly watched, by someone I know. I feel like I know them well. I know that I probably do not know them, but I shall find out who did it. Correction, we shall find out who has been watching us, if someone has been watching us at all. I have never seen them. Never. Hopefully, I will never see them.

I think I'm about to be betrayed by someone I know well.

Chapter 17

"So… Where do we start," Richard said, while leaning on a tree in the forest, playing around with the materials that we had bought,
"We need a plot o' land." I said, my accent naturally changing from a standard American accent to a mild British accent. It happens, I say something in an accent that isn't my standard, usually for emphasis, or by complete accident. This time it was just an accident. I will change that. Soon, I will change that. I will try to be constant in one accent, standard American.

For the plot of land, I had bought some old 100-dollar bills, from the mid 1930's. I will go to the 1980's and buy it with a fake ID or I'd do it under the name of my great-grandmother. She would be glad to see her great-grandchild. There is also a lot of family resemblance between me and her. But I would need to be careful. Very careful. I should not let anything bad happen in the past, or else, I might not exist. The "Grandfather Paradox" would happen.

But a fake ID might also work, but I'd need to pay property taxes, and I don't want to have to deal with the fake ID.

My great-grandmother is alive in the present day, at the age of 89.
So I'm going to go with the first option.
Time to meet some relatives.

I will take a trip to 1980. I needed to take a quick stop at home though. Present day home. A very quick stop. I needed to grab some supplies.

I needed to tell an impossible story in the most convincing way.

"You're gonna go back in time to 1980 and convince your great-grandmother that you are her great-grandson and that you need a plot of land for an emergency? It took me a lot of evidence to convince me that you were telling the truth when you came to take me into the future. Won't it be harder for you to convince your Great-grandmother without any evidence?" Richard's mother said, baffled.

"I'm going to get evidence from the present," I said, knowing that what I was doing was right. "Okay..." Both Richard and his mother said, dragging the last letter to make it have around 4 syllables.

"Do you want me to leave you here? I'll be quick." I said to Richard and his mom.

"We'll come with you," Richard said, scared enough to probably faint.

"I'll only be gone for a second," I told him. His face relaxed quite a bit.

 I left them there.

'Tis time to tell a tremendously tall tale.

Chapter 18

So again, I felt dead and lifeless while time traveling, for a few seconds, and after that I was back home. I grabbed the family photo album, took photocopies of every single photo in it, and took some dollar bills that were from the present day. I also learned everything I could about my great-grandmother. I took a calculator, which would be considered "a very big technological advancement" back in 1980.

I was off, going far into the past, again having the weird time travel feeling, lifelessness and blankness.

1980 felt... nice. I noticed that the air seemed fresher, and the city was way less crowded. More trees. Definitely more trees. I had my great-grandmother's address. I walked, and walked, and walked some more. I looked at all the shops which seemed old yet so new. The stuff in the stores seemed so new. They looked like new antiques. It was the best way to describe them: new antiques.

Everyone was looking at me like I was an alien. An odd man with a strange shade of blue eyes and dyed green hair came up to me and said, "Kid, are you okay? Are you lost? Are you mentally well? How many fingers am I holding up?" he said, with two skinny fingers sticking up.

"Twenty? Maybe thirty, give or take some," I said, controlling my laughter and I shoved past him and walked away. He seemed like a good man, although I wanted to mess with him a bit, because he also seemed a bit rude.

I continued to navigate myself around Denver, but more and more people looked at me strangely. After around 60 people looked at me weirdly, due to the 21st century clothes and whatnot, I went to the nearest clothing store.

I went into the store and asked a worker what the latest trend is as of now, and he looked at me from my feet to my head, and back, and decided not to question my appearance. He pointed to some clothes and said one word to me: "There." I picked out something that seemed alright and I took it and went up to the cashier. "That'll be 5.50 kid, you definitely need the outfit, you look like you've designed and made your own clothes or something like that. Where are they from anyway?" I had to think fast.

"Ummmm... Costa Rica?" I said. "Or no. I think it may have been Russia, or Germany. Possibly China. My family travels a lot sir, so it is very hard to recall where these clothes are from." I told him. He bought the story. As I was handing him 6 dollars he said, "I understand, well, see you around, kid!"

"Keep the change, and have a great day." I said and walked out, but turned around for a second, and what I saw was not what I had expected. I saw him smile, and that was much anticipated.

But his smile was crooked, as though he were the last one alive on this planet. I had a bad feeling I knew this guy, and he knew something I did not.

Chapter 19

My whole body began to shake. My feet were moving without my control. They made me walk back into the store without my will. I told my feet to walk the other way, but they would not listen. I went up to the cashier.

"Are you by any chance Frederick Z.T.?" I asked him, knowing the answer to this would most likely be yes.

"Well yeah, why do you ask?" He asked, with that knowing look in his eyes. "I'm related to you," I told him. "Well yeah, you look exactly like me. How are you related to me exactly?" he said, smiling.
"I'm your grandson," I said. My feet were turning into jelly.

"I'm not that old, now tell me kid, who are you to me," he told me, annoyed. I had to manage the situation somehow.

"I'm your second cousin once removed." This was a bit crazy to tell my grandfather, but I will go with it. "No… You are not. Definitely not." He said, getting increasingly angry by the second. I sprinted out of the place, because I did not want to risk anything happening to me. But I did leave a photo. It was captured on my 12th birthday, with him, my mom, and me. He will know the truth.

I turned back to see if there was anyone following me. To my relief, there were not any angry people chasing me. Now I had to go to his mom's house. But I needed to change into my "new" old clothes. I changed behind a dumpster in a place that did not have many people walking around, and the people who did walk by did not notice me at all.

My "old" new clothes were not useful at that point, so I gave them to a random person, and he looked at me in confusion, and walked on, looking at the weird looking clothes in his hands.

I now went and asked around for where the address was located. The G.P.S. system had been invented, but it was only used for military purposes at that time. I could've gotten a map, but I had decided not to have any more encounters with 80's people that may recognize me, although this was unlikely, I just wanted to be on the safe side.

I walked and asked people and walked and asked more people and made progress with the trip. The reason why I did not use the time machine was due to me not knowing the exact coordinates for the house, I only had the address, and the street would have had many name changes in forty years. The last person I asked for directions told me this.

"Kid, go straight, turn right at the first right, then left at the second left, and you will see a house that will be blue with an orange door. Go 3 blocks down from that and you will arrive at your destination." She walked on. I thanked her. The instructions were quite long but clear. Finally, I was at my great-grandmother's home. I knocked. Once. Twice. The third time I knocked I heard a voice, calling out to me.

"Come in!!"

Chapter 20

Have you ever had those days when you've had to see a family member 43 years in the past? Hopefully, you have not; I certainly think that if you could do something like that then the world is in grave danger. A person with a time machine could be extremely dangerous, and they could practically rule the world.

It would be crazy if time machines actually existed. Between me as a novel character to you, a reader, I just wanted to tell you that time machines could either make humanity great, or make it go extinct instantly. Hopefully in this story nobody finds out about my time machine, as if they do, we may go extinct, or at least everyone in this story.

So I walked into my great-grandmother's home, shutting the door behind me. She was standing near the stove, making some kind of stew or soup. It smelled wonderful and the aroma of it was pulling me near the pot. I was scared my legs would not listen to me, but this time, they did, thankfully.

"I want to talk to you," I told my great-grandmother.

"Have a seat, little child, have a seat. I'll be with you in a second," she said, tasting the soup with a metal spoon, reaching to her left to grab some salt.

I went to the living room and sat on a chair, waiting for my great-grandmother to come. I looked around. I saw that there were some photos hanging on the wall in picture frames, with photos of her and some relatives that I did not know. I waited for a few minutes. I heard the door open and close. I turned, and I saw that my grandfather was there. He came here after his store closed. We established eye contact, and he was just as shocked to see me as I was to see him. He pretended like I was not there, and he walked on, into the kitchen, probably to talk to his mom. He then came out of the kitchen and went upstairs, and still ignored the fact that I was there.

My great-grandmother came out of the kitchen and said, "Child, do you want stew?"
Did I? Of course I did.
"Yes please!" I said to her, very cheerfully, as if the feeling that I was going to drink stew had given me the same amount of energy I would have gotten if I had actually drank some 'til my stomach was full.

She brought a bowl with stew in it and sat near me. "What did you come here for?" She asked. My stew was too hot to drink, so I did not drink it yet, and I let it sit. "What if I told you that I was your great-grandson. Would you believe me?" I asked her.

"No dear, I'm not that old yet." She laughed. I realized the stew seemed cool enough to drink, so I took a big sip out of it.

"I have evidence." I said, my voice was starting to slur, and I felt a bit more sleepy than usual.

"Like what?" She said, curious.

"Photos," I said, pointing to the bag in my hand. My consciousness was slipping out of me, like a soap bar on a wet bathtub. I fell to the side, groggily.

 My great-grandmother stood above me and smiled with self-pride.

"Did you enjoy your stew, dear?" Was the last thing she said before I fainted.

Betrayed.

Something tells me this isn't the last time that'll happen.

Chapter 21

When I woke up, I figured I was in the basement.

I felt dizzy and weird and all at the same time. The light was on, and my great-grandmother was sitting there.

"It's about time you wake up. Are you actually who you say you are?" My great-grandmother asked me. "Yes, Grandma, yes I am." I said, hoping she would believe me.

"I will let you go, as long as you explain what all your things are, and one wrong move, and you are done for." she said, holding up the bag that I had brought with me. I agreed to tell her more about it. I laid out the contents of the bag on the floor, the calculator, and some dollar bills. I finally put the photos on the floor, laying them out one by one, my great-grandmother peering over my shoulder, and my grandfather close behind her.

"What is this thing?" my great-grandmother said, while picking up the calculator.

"It is a calculator! Don't you all have calculators now?" I said. My grandfather stepped in.

"Yeah we do, I see them a lot. Although I have never seen one so complex before." I then told them to play around with it. They did, for a bit. They then put it down and looked at the dollar bills. The dollar bills were just standard 1-dollar bills, and on them they had SERIES 2017 on them. They were both shocked by this. "Can I please keep this," my grandfather whined. "Nope, I do not want to change the past in any way." I told them both.

"So, you are from the future? What year?" My great-grandmother said.

"Yes, and I am from 2024," I said, knowing that I had finally earned their trust. Finally, they turned their attention toward the photos.

They saw photos of their old selves. They were both extremely shocked. My grandfather fainted. "Who knows when he'll awaken. Do you have water?" I asked. "I'll be right back with some."

My great-grandmother walked up the stairs, coming back with a glass of water in her hands, and poured it all on my grandfather in haste, who woke up quite quickly. I then explained all the photos. My grandfather gave me the photo that I had given him. "I honestly thought it was a prank!" He said, giving me the picture. "Do you know why I came here?" I told them. "Why?" Both the mother and son said, in perfect synchronization.
"I have a deal to strike with you."

Chapter 22

"I need a plot of land in the Colorado forest, and I will pay for it," I said, holding up the old 100-dollar bills. "Take it, take it all, but I need a plot of land from you, and you have to pay property taxes. Register it under grandma's ID, as she will be alive in the present, so you would not have to buy it in your name grandpa." I said, and after that, my grandfather made a strange face, and said, "So will I not be alive in your time?"

"It's because you're too much of a blabbermouth! You cannot keep a simple secret! Mom's birthday party was ruined because of you! But yes, you will be alive. I do not want you to tell anyone that your mom owns land in the forest. If it were your land, you would tell someone immediately. Please, do not tell anyone. Do not tell anyone I was here.

Please do not tell anyone about the land. It may change the future forever."

My grandfather seemed offended. I quickly apologized to him, and he looked better. "I will come back after a few years, and check on you all, and see where the land is. I think all the money should cover any costs associated with land buying and property taxes that you will face in the land buying process. Do you have a day that I could come?" I said, and waited for a reply. "March 9, 1984" My great-grandmother said. I got up, and realized the time machine was not there.

I looked around for the time machine. "Where is that gray briefcase? It helps me travel through time." asked, worried. "We tried opening it with a hammer. It's upstairs. Frederick! Get it please!" My great-grandmother shouted. I started to panic, and I started to walk in circles. My grandfather ran up the stairs. I was going round and round and round and round and… My grandfather came back with a steel briefcase. It was perfectly unharmed. Not even a dent. I think the internal parts should also be quite good as the outside seems fine to me. I picked up all the photos, and I walked upstairs.

My great-grandmother and my grandfather followed me. "Well, I really need to go, like, right now." I said. "To the bathroom?" My grandfather said, pointing the opposite way to where I was going, as that is where the bathroom was. "No, to 1984, to check on you all and the land and whatnot" I said, holding back a laugh. "Well, I guess, I'll see you in… what like, 4 years from now?" My grandfather said, "Yep, ummm, bye…" I said opening the time machine briefcase, and everyone watched as it unfolded itself, technology at its maximum.

"But dear, you did not finish your stew," My great-grandmother said, with what looked a lot like genuine sorrow on her face. I had to laugh at that. Everyone laughed. I stepped into the time machine, my head was still outside, and I gave them some financial advice. "In September of 1985, a company called Apple will have its shares go down to 7 cents. Invest in it then. Buy 1000$ worth of it. It will make your son retire as a millionaire." They were shocked. "Will do, kid, will do." My grandfather said. I went in the time machine and set the time to 1984 and I went.

Time to meet my mother.

Chapter 23

So I went forward around 4 years in time, I felt happy, yet I could not feel the happiness while traveling in time. I felt dead... again. Time travel is the weirdest feeling ever. It is something that can only be felt by those who do it. Dead is the only word that can come close to it. The feeling of painless death while being alive. Just going completely blank, but knowing what is around you, and what you are doing.

I finally arrived. 1984 seemed... The same as 1980, actually. So I came out of the machine, which was in the living room. I was happy to find my great-grandmother there, with a baby in her hands. She smiled when I got out of the machine. "Greetings! I was expecting you! Do you want some stew? I swear it is not drugged," she said, getting up to grab a bowl.

I looked at the child and immediately knew who it was. "So, what do you call my mom?" I asked, curiously. "M.D." My great-grandmother said. "M.D." I called out, and a second later, the child looked up. She looked to be around a year old. "Hewwwwo," My mom said, smiling.

My great-grandmother brought me stew, exactly like the stew I had been drugged with. "Could you please take a picture of this?" I asked my great-grandmother, while picking my mom up, and making the toddler sit on my lap. She said that she would, and she brought a camera. I smiled and let the flash blind my eyes. She gave me the photo that she had taken. I put it away and put my mom back on the couch, took a sip of goat stew, and went right into business.

"Where is the land located?" She gave me a map and it had the exact location of the plot. I thanked her for the stew, which I had finished quite quickly.

I also thanked them for the land, and also for just believing the most absurd yet true story possible. "So where is Grandma and Grandpa?" I asked my great-grandmother, and she responded.

"They are at the store, buying some stuff." I knew what was going to happen today,

"They will suffer a car accident today, and break a bone or two, but I promise that they will remain alive and well." I told her, in sorrow. She was shocked. I made her calm down and told her again that they would be safe.

I'd heard that on a Friday in March my grandparents went to the store and left the child behind and had a car accident. I could have bet money that it was today. I could bet anything I have that it is going to be today, because they almost always take their child anywhere they go. Anywhere. They loved my mother very much.

I made my great-grandmother calm down and I said, "They will be safe," and I turned around and went into the time machine. Before going in, I smiled and waved. My mom was sucking her thumb at the time, and yelled "bbbbyyye," stressing the b and the y very hard, as if it was meant to be pronounced like that, typical baby behavior. I went in, setting the date to the day I left Richard and his mother in the forest. I set it to the exact second that I had left.

Now I am going to build an underground bunker.

Chapter 24

Lifelessness, yet again.

I'm starting to get sick of time travel. Imagine this: You are given a whole box of one hundred lollipops to finish. You must finish it all within 2 hours. The first five to ten lollipops will taste great and sweet, and you will enjoy it. From ten to twenty-five it will feel less and less enjoyable, and finally the last seventy-five lollipops will taste horrible, and you will hate eating it and it will seem as boring as doing laundry or raking the yard. Eating lollipops would seem like a chore after doing it too much. Also, you might harm your digestive system or your teeth if you eat too many lollipops. Correction, you WILL harm it.

I feel like time travel is like that, except without harm. It is mostly just boredom. The lifeless feeling.

I was back, two years from the present, in a forest. Richard's face was in shock and happiness. "Denver! You were only gone for like... One second!! I didn't even have time to blink!" He exclaimed. I smiled and said,

"Technology, Richard, technology." I said, grinning. "So where is the plot of land located?" Richard's mom asked. "Follow me!" I said, walking while looking at the map. So we walked, and walked, and walked some more. We walked through an endless terrain of green and brown and more green and brown with the occasional yellow here and there. Wild fruits grew, and every step made deer prance away in fear. We had finally reached our destination.

Luckily, there seemed to be less vegetation in this area. There were not any trees, and it seemed like a little hidden clearing. I had brought my hole digging robot that I had built when I was 8 (for attempting to dig to the core, it did not work though.) I programmed the robot to dig a 15 feet by 15 feet by 9 feet hole in the ground.

I let the machine do its work, taking the soil, compressing it, and launching it, and pellets of hardness were raining from the sky. It was taking a while, so I showed Richard the photo that was taken with my mom. He laughed, stating that I looked exactly like her. The pellets hit our heads a lot, and I decided to go back to where we had left our stuff and transport it using the time machine. So, I went to the place and started teleporting back and forth, from here to there, and from there to here.

This was going to be a long day.

Chapter 25

I cannot stress how much I hate time travel. But I did it like a chore over and over and over again. It was tiring, and very boring.

But I did it. I did it to help another person live well. Saving lives is the equivalent to breathing now. Finally, I was done with the transportation of the materials, and I had gotten the septic tank from the house, which I will not discuss for now (or maybe ever). All the building materials were in a pile, a big pile, and it was very organized. The hole was ready, and we put a steel frame in. Next, we did the plumbing, and put the walls in. It was tough. Very tough. But I had 6 hands working, and occasionally some mouths and feet here and there. I did some wiring (I know, I know, I am such a geek. I learned how to do it in a construction course online. Simple, yet hard.) I connected the wires to the main power source, the rechargeable batteries. Richard and his mother were working on making the bathrooms. I had given them a mini lesson on how to do it, so they should be fine. I am currently letting my hole digging robot dig down deep, until it makes a well, and I will use that water.

A while later...

   All the wiring and plumbing is complete. Now I will move on to making the insides look nice. We put tiles and put them on a cool looking floor. It looked nice. Very nice. It is pretty good. We moved on to the kitchen. I put in a microwave, a mini fridge, and an electric stove. Now all we had to do was get groceries. I told Richard's mom to make a list of things that she needed, and I stepped into the time machine, used the teleportation feature, and went to the store. I got everything she needed and came back. I gave everything to her. I was planning on doing this again and again, time traveling every week, for two years (more than one hundred weeks) and it seemed very efficient. The bunker was accessible by a hidden hatch. The top of the bunker was sealed in by dirt. I went into the bunker and stood there for a bit, amazed by it, wondering how I designed such a wonderful place. We'd worked out that Richard's mom will make art to sell to cover the cost of the bunker. So everything was figured out. I came out of the bunker, and just then, I saw a person run. He was wearing a black face mask. What was more strange was that I think I knew him from somewhere.

Anyway...

We have a stalker.

Chapter 26

I sprinted after him, a rock in my hand as a weapon. I was 20 feet behind him. Adrenaline was kicking in, and it was just about as helpful as my right hand, only, my right hand was a tiny bit more helpful, because it had a rock in it, which would be helpful any second now. I ran, the gap between us getting smaller and smaller. The person turned back once, although I did not get a good look at his face, and plus, a mask was covering it. Right then, the most unexpected thing happened. I tripped on my shoelace.

You know, sometimes the best of plots can be foiled by something as simple as a shoelace. Folks, prevent all preventable accidents. The man continued to run. I got up, knowing that it was impossible to catch up to him. He was at least 30 feet away now so I did what I knew would never work. I threw the rock as hard as I could, making sure to aim for the head. It was a total accident, but it hit him on the back, and he fell down, whimpering in pain. I took another rock, which was quite big, and I sneaked up behind the person, who was on his knees, and tossed it right on his head. He fell to the side, either unconscious, or dead. Hopefully the former.

I made him lay on his back and removed his face mask. You would be shocked to know who it was.... Really shocked...

Chapter 27

In two words, the best way to put it is this: Nasty betrayal. I'll tell you later who it is. Now I have to deal with him. He seemed to be alive. In fact, he seemed to be quite well, and I noticed that his eyes were still open. Right at that second, I heard another pair of footsteps fleeing from the place and turned toward the sound. Think back, think back to why this all happened. Infer, reader, infer. Infer, for those who infer can get more information out of one sentence than not inferring through the whole book. Think back and infer. Infer.

So, I let the man run, because if he did not run, I would not be here.

So he ran, and did not turn back, and I thought about what to do about the person in front of me. I was around 200 feet away from my bunker. I held him by the feet and dragged him. It took me a while, around 5 minutes to drag a bunch of dead weight through rough forest terrain.

I had to lift him at certain places, due to the fallen trees. He was not too heavy, but it was still ridiculously hard to lift him, due to him being dead weight. So, I came to the bunker, and I went into the bunker. Something did not feel right. I got some rope, and I dragged the person inside the bunker, and I tied his hands and feet up. Something still did not seem right. I looked around, trying to figure out what was wrong. I knew what was wrong now.
Richard and his mother were gone.

The Author, who I had tied up, smiled, and said, "You did not expect this twist, did you? You won't get them back. You will never get them back UNLESS I want to. So, start behaving."

"Why did you come here?" I asked, confused. "For a plot twist, duh. Anyway, I'm still on your side. I just want to make the story more exciting!" He said, while attempting to untie the knots.

"You can't untie 'em. It is an extremely strong knot." I said, impressed with the amount of random knowledge I had. I knew random facts and did courses on stuff that would never be useful in real life, and learned skills that could only benefit me in the oddest of situations, like this one. "Are you going to untie me, or should I do it myself?" he asked, quite annoyed and angry. "Try to untie it," I said, quite happy that I could get revenge for the person who makes me work for him with no salary. I make the story go by excitingly, but I get nothing in return. "Look, I can do anything in this book, look at all the blood and bruises from the rock. It shall vanish. Watch this knot. It will untie itself. Look at that piece of paper, it will hover for 6 seconds. Anything I think is possible," he said, while all the things he described had happened. "So... Are you going to be holding a grudge against me for the rock and tying you up here?" I asked, partially in fear, but mostly just curiosity. "Nope, that is water under a bridge now. Plus, I'm only a character in a book. I feel no pain. My pain is all just paper and ink. Also, it was a really exciting way to end a chapter, almost killing a person, and finding out who they were. That was amazing. So now I know what has happened to Richard and his mom. The question is: Do you know what happened to him, and how will you figure it out?" The Author said. He seemed to be telling the truth, and I really did think he forgave me.

"So Denver, are you ready to play a little game? It's called 'Find the missing people' and I think you can handle it."

Chapter 28

I thought about what I should do. I could take fingerprints, but I would not know where to start, or even if fingerprints would be helpful. As far as I know, they could be hiking in the forest. So I had to make a logical plan. A plan that should be complicated, yet simple to do.

I had just the plan.

"So... I am going to set the time to a few minutes ago. I am going to set the place to a tree right above the base. Do you want to come with me?" I told The Author, who replied, "Since this involves spying from the trees, sure, why not!" We both were sent back in time, to only a few minutes ago. We were sent to the tree, and there, it was the perfect spot. The time machine was wedged between two trees, and we had a perfect view of what was going on beneath us. I first saw myself run. I saw myself trip, and get back up, and throw the rock. It was cool, watching myself do everything. Now we both had our eyes on the bunker. I watched and watched, waiting for something to happen. We waited for a good 10 minutes, and I saw myself drag The Author into the bunker. "Did we miss something?" I asked The Author, who did not seem surprised by this. "We have to get down from this tree right now." The Author said. I made the time machine portable by pressing a button. It turned into a briefcase, and I climbed down with it, and The Author also climbed down, and he was a few feet above me. We finally reached the ground. If the ground were small enough, I would have hugged it, but the best I could do was lay down on my stomach and stretch my arms out. It was hard staying on a tree for ten minutes. Try it one day.

We went into the bunker, and looked around, and said, "They've got to be here somewhere."

Chapter 29

We searched the place. It did not seem likely for such a small space to have a hiding spot. We checked every potential hiding spot. I even checked in the fridge, knowing that they would not be there, but I did it for the feeling of completing my task. I was about to check underneath the carpets when The Author shouted, "Hey Denver, get over here right now! Bring a hammer!" He was in the bathroom, fiddling with the mirror. "Please give that to me." He said, pointing at the hammer. I was surprised. The Author never says please. I knew something was going on right now. He took the hammer, and carefully and swiftly smashed the mirror (I still do not know how that was possible, carefully and swiftly smashing something.) For all of you who are superstitious, sorry but I cannot help you. After he broke the mirror, I saw that there was around 2 feet of dirt, and after that, there was a hollow room. The mirror was a lot more than it seemed on the outside. A lot more. The best explanation was that there was a secret underground bunker already built here, right next to the one we made. I heard footsteps from inside. I also heard the sound of crying, laughter, and boredom (which usually does not have a sound, but in this case, it was the sound of someone yawning). In the other bunker, I saw that almost every missing person from this area who had not yet been found was over here. In that place, I saw Richard and his mother talking to some of the people there.

The Author looked at me and said, "Plot twist!"

We crawled into the place where the mirror used to be. I went to Richard and asked him about what was going on. "Richard! What happened!" I yelled. "We heard a weird noise from the other side of the mirror, so we took it off, dug a bit, and we found this place. After that we put the mirror back in its place from the other side. It was really hard to do in ten minutes," Richard said. "That does not sound very believable, Richard. How did you put the mirror back?" I asked. "I just shoved it right back where it belonged, and it stuck!" He said, worried that I might not believe him. "Did you try pulling the mirror off?" I asked The Author. "Nope, I thought it would be more dramatic if I smashed the mirror with a hammer. I knew I could have just pulled it off, but I wanted to feel the glass explode all around me. You've broken glass like that before, right?" The Author said. "Nope," I lied. He knew that I was lying. I looked around the place. Most of the people who went missing around this area who were never found in the last two years were here. They were all just random people. Well, we came here to save one life.

Now we have at least 25 to save.

Chapter 30

Interrogation is very hard, especially when you do not know where to begin. I went to our bunker and grabbed a paper and a pencil. "Ummmmm... What is your name?" I asked a teenage boy. "Why do you need to know that? I choose to remain silent." the teen said. I should probably just leave him here to die. If you are ever in a situation like that, please cooperate with the people trying to save you. "Tell me your name or I will leave you here to rot and stink and be eaten by worms." The last part was what I think got his attention. He looked at me furiously. "Braden Park," he said, in extreme anger. "So, Park, cooperate, and anyone who does not cooperate will be left here. So how did you get here?" I said, frustrated by the stupidity of this kid. "I was walking down the street on my way home from school when suddenly a gray SUV came, and its license plate number was HGJ-1 and 2 more numbers that I forgot. Someone in a mask came out of the car and made me inhale chloroform. When I was conscious, I realized that I was in here, with no way out, I mean, until now," he said, and saying it made him calmer. He was definitely way less angry. "When were you brought here?" I asked, this time a bit more kindly. "Just around a week ago." He said. "What state was the vehicle from?" I asked. "Here, it was from Colorado," he said. "Okay, next person, come here!" I said, while jotting everything down. I interrogated everyone in the room. I found that everyone had similar experiences. I noticed that the other bunker seemed kind of large, and possibly well built. It also had a lot of things in it and was sort of... good, as if the person who made it wanted to make it comfortable. It seemed odd that somebody would make a bunker right next to ours, and that we did not notice it. During the interrogation, I found that everyone was kidnapped using the same license plate, and that the fifth digit was 4. Nobody remembered the last digit, and that seemed strange, but then again, it isn't something you would be thinking about while being kidnapped. So, I gathered all the information, and organized it. I let everyone go into our bunker and opened the hatch, where everyone stepped outside for a while, and after a moment of fresh air, I made them go back inside. Now I had to deal with a bunch of missing people. They all went inside, and I made them go back into the bunker they had come from. There was a kidnapper out there, and it was my duty to find him.

"No way are you going to find a kidnapper. It's way too dangerous. I shouldn't have become an author. I should've become a firefighter or a pilot, or maybe a game show host. This job is annoying. I would not have to have to deal with people like you," he said, worried that I'll die in the process of finding the kidnapper, which was quite possibly true, but I will do it anyway.

I got out of the bunker and searched for the other bunker's opening. After a quick search of the place, I found the opening. It was hidden underneath a rock, a big rock. I examined their bunker opening. It was designed well, and it seemed like it could only be opened by the outside and could not be opened from the inside. One way opening. Very clever. I found a lock, which was opened by a key. Three simple words: I picked it. It's funny, how I casually say I picked a lock from a secret underground bunker that has 25 kidnapped people in it. It is very funny. I picked it and opened it, revealing the bunker. So I had found the opening, and I had found a ton of missing people. Now I had no clue on how to get these people back home safely without exposing my identity, which in my opinion is much greater than these people's lives, because if they knew that I could time travel, they would confiscate my time machine and kill me, and change the fate of the world. They will destroy the world. I think the lives of billions of people are much more important than these 25. I will do my part though. I will do what I can to save these people without exposing myself, but if not, the sad truth is, I'm going to be forced to leave them all here to die.

Chapter 31

Now I have to think. If I want to save all these people without exposing myself, I'm going to have to plan this out perfectly. I had a risky plan in mind. One that involves possible death. I called Richard, his mother, and The Author in for a quick chat. "Look I don't have much time, make this quick. I need to write the sequel for this book." The Author said, impatiently. "Okay, look, I've got a plan," I told everyone, whose eyes got brighter, and their ears and heads were tilted closer to me, ready to listen. "So we need to find the kidnapper, or kidnappers. How do we do it? Well, we need bait. We need to lure them in. Richard's mother was going to be kidnapped. We stopped them from taking her by coming here and doing this. We need to let her get kidnapped. We need to let the person kidnap her. We need to track this person.

We will find this person and *kill them*," I said, confidently. "I don't think we need to take it that far, but I think we get the point. Now how are we going to do this?" Richard said, worried that I might do something horrible. "Look Denver, this book is meant for kids from the ages of 10-14. I think murder is a bit too... violent for people of that age." The Author said, worried about his readers. "But I won't kill him brutally. I'll just shoot him with a bit too many tranquilizer darts and make him die of an overdose. After that, I'll put the body in the bunker and burn the bunker down. Nobody will notice a bit of smoke in the middle of a forest in Colorado." I said, pleading to kill them, whoever they may be. "Well, that seems reasonable. Go ahead. Call me if you need any help. I am going to work on this story's sequel." The Author said, while sitting at a small table in the bunker and tapping his pen on the table, in no particular way. Just random taps. I plotted out a devious plan to catch the person. We needed some supplies to do all this. Time for a trip to the store. Remember that location tracker that I bought and said that it would be useful in the future? Well now, it would be useful, but we need 3 more. We would also need some other things.

We are going to buy some simple spy gear. Some of this stuff will need to be bought online, like spy cameras, whereas some of the things can be bought at a regular store. So first I ordered everything I needed online and went to the place where I usually pick up my packages by making myself go 2 days later using the time machine. So, I got the spy cameras. The spy cameras were very small, and they were hidden inside a button. I told everyone to wear one at all times and turn it on when they feel like they are in danger. So now we needed some walkie talkies, just for fun. We all went to the store and saw some walkie talkies for sale at a reasonable price. I took them and walked up to the cashier. "That'd be $52.64 please, is that going to be cash or card." The cashier said. "Card,"

The Author said, while taking a card out from his back pocket. He waved it inches from the cashier's face. "Wait! You're..." The cashier said, and he fainted or died, honestly, I had no clue. "What did you do to him!" I yelled. "I showed him my book character identification card. Check your pockets, you all should have one too." The Author said, smiling. I checked my pockets, and so did the others. I am surprised none of us noticed this. We all had book character identification cards. I read mine.

Name: Denver Colorado
Role: Protagonist
Characteristics: Smart, funny, and nerdy.
Hobbie(s): Chemistry, Learning random facts.
Other fact(s): Very good at subtle humor.

I also looked at the other IDs.

Name: The Author

Role: Side character

Characteristics: Smart, clever, and smart

Hobbie(s): Writing, picking on book characters.

Other fact(s): Can control any character as he pleases.

Name: Richard James

Role: Side character

Characteristics: Stupid, cooperative, kind

Hobbie(s): Badminton

Other fact(s): Sucks his thumb when nobody's looking.

The last ID was what caught me off guard.

Name: Sally James

Role: WILL BE REVEALED NEAR CLIMAX

Characteristics: Clever, Smart, Sneaky

Hobbie(s): Puzzles

Other fact(s): Has never thanked Denver for saving her. Big secret about her will be revealed in the climax.

I looked at Mrs. James. "I only know what you know, only he knows what is going to happen to us in the future." She said, pointing up. The Author was hovering a foot above her. "Yeah, that's true," he said, holding back laughter. Mrs. James looked up and got angry and yelled, "I didn't mean you! I meant go—" The Author interrupted her. "We get it! Do you always have to ruin a good joke!" Now I guess I had to divert them all. "Guys! We have to use our time wisely. Let's get going!" I said, which really worked out. "But what about the things! We need to pay!" Richard said. "It's on the house." The Author said, grinning. We took the things which felt wrong, taking stuff without paying. I would *NEVER* do something like that. Yeah, I would never, and I have never done anything like that.

Most of you would be like "RIIIIIGHT...." but still, the employee paid for that thing which I had gotten with the -100% tip trick. Now we had some spy gear, and some cool stuff. So now, we can start our mission.

A mission to save the lives of dozens of people.

Chapter 32

We did some tests with the spy gear. I tested out the spy cameras to see if they all worked. The cameras also had microphones to record stuff via audio. "Is everyone ready for some espionage?" I asked everyone. The three of them said yes in their own ways. Richard said "Yep!!" His mom said "Yes." The Author said "Affirmative." And finally, I squealed "YAY!!" in a really high-pitched voice. I had filled the hole in our mirror with dirt again because I had opened the hatch so the alternative route to the other bunker was not needed. Another reason why I had to close it was because we needed the bathroom there. We needed privacy! So, I covered it up and fixed the wall on their side and the mirror on ours, and I packed the hole with dirt. The place was as good as it was before. I had a good idea on what the plan was. I am going to time travel to Richard's house and drop his mom off where we picked her up at the exact time we picked her up. I would then make her do what she was about to do, which was to take a quick walk outside. She will most likely be kidnapped. After that, I will confront the kidnapper. Confrontation should be easy; I will bring a tranquilizer dart gun and I will shoot him down if he tries to do anything. In fact, I am going to make a dart that goes into the body but only releases the anesthetic when I push a button, so that it will make it easier to take down the enemy. I started to design it. I was done with the design for the dart. I made a few, and it took a while. I love inventing and chemistry. I also like construction. There is a story on how I started loving chemistry. Once, I was a child, and I saw some chemicals. I took them and made something amazing with them. My mother saw this and bought anything to support my passion. I soon started making great inventions. She loved it, until one day, not too long ago, I made an explosive with bananas, hence, a banana bomb. I extracted the potassium from it and made it explode by putting it in water. It made anything within a ten-foot radius explode. I was around 20 feet away. Then she started restricting my inventions.

The dart I just made was both inventing and chemistry, because I would need to calculate the amount of anesthesia to take to not kill a person (or kill them) and the inventing part was the dart itself. Simple, yet so complex. Now it is time for some time travel. Richard's mother, The Author, and I went into the time machine. The reason why Richard could not come was because there was a possibility that he would bump into himself in his house. In fact, he definitely WILL bump into himself, causing who knows what. I went and dropped them off at the exact second that I will leave, so that I would not bump into my time traveling self. So, we all went in, and the time traveling phenomenon happened, where we all felt dead for a bit. I dropped off Richard's mother and I made The Author follow her and keep track of her. I then went back to the second I left Richard at the bunker, and I picked up Richard. We both went a bit farther away than the house so that Richard would not bump into himself. I temporarily dyed my hair so that if I bump into myself my past self won't notice. The sun was high in the sky, shining brightly, with some clouds passing over it every now and then. I don't know if I'll see it shine after today. Who knows what will happen to me in the span of a couple hours.

This may be my last day.

Chapter 33

So, we were all set, ready to face what would happen in the span of an hour or two. We followed Richard's mother from a good distance, waiting for something to happen. I made this time go by faster by talking to Richard. "So, Richard, tell me about your life." I asked. This was one of the first times in my life that I had asked this question. I rarely ask questions about other people's lives. "It's nice. I have good friends, and I have quite a bit of money; I have 500 dollars!" He said. "Well, money isn't really that important at this age. Look, we could die any second now. Any second. You can't save your life with money, usually." I said. "Stay positive Denver, stay positive. Okay, wanna check on mom with the walkie talkie." He said, while taking his walkie talkie out of his pocket and continued, "Mom, come in mom. Is everything alright? Does anything seem suspicious?" The walkie talkie (practically) came to life and said, "Yeah, everything is fine, over-and-out." He put the walkie talkie back in his pocket, and asked me "Denver, have you ever told me about your father?" Richard asked. "Richard, have I not told you the story before?" I asked him back. "No." he told me. "Well, it is a story for another day," I said, quite surprised that I have not told him before. We spoke for a while, but right then a gray SUV came, and used some kind of anesthetic and took Richard's mother and put her in the back, all in less than 8 seconds. We were about 300 feet away. The SUV passed by us, we pretended that we were not looking, and the driver did not notice. I quickly took my location tracker out. Coincidentally, there was a house with two bicycles by the front. I knocked on the door. An old woman opened the door. Upon seeing us she said "I won't donate any money. I won't buy cookies from you. I won't join your religion." I then said, "No, no. Could I borrow those bicycles? Here, I'll give you $200." I took 2 hundred-dollar bills from my back pocket, and upon seeing the money, she snatched it and told us that we could.

I took the bicycles and started looking at the location tracker and we both went in the way that was the quickest way to get there. We both pedaled at the fastest pace that we could. My heart was pumping so fast. We pedaled for at least ten minutes, until we were behind the car. We maintained a good gap from the car and followed it from a good distance. We chased the car down, and we were careful not to let the car notice us. We followed the car down the streets of Denver until the car stopped and a guy in a mask came out of it. We slowed down. He then looked straight at us. He was walking toward us. Busted.

Chapter 34

"Well, well, well, it's Richard James and Denver Colorado, what a pleasure it is to be seeing you. Denver, I love the hair dye, you should keep it. So, what brings you here?" The man said. "I.. ummmm .. you.." I started stuttering very badly. It was very awkward to be speechless. Off topic: I am not going to keep my hair dyed. Knowing I might need to make him pass out, I took my remote injection darts and shot one at him. He didn't even notice the dart going in. I then started talking. "So, who are you? Your voice sounds familiar."

"It is for me to know and you to find out."

"Why do you kidnap people?" I asked, and my body was trembling in fear. I inched closer and closer to him, and now the gap between him and me was only ten feet.

  "I kidnap people who are directly responsible for a person's death." He said.

"Ohhh, so you are just kidnapping murderers." I told him.

"Yes, indeed I am. You know Braden Park, right? Well, he was a drug dealer at his high school, and he gave something to a guy and that guy died of an overdose. The police never found him, they didn't even try finding out who it was, and they didn't even care. For them, it was just another foolish teen. I honestly have nothing against police officers, if they work hard, they can be very good people. These police officers didn't care. But I cared. I found out who did it and did this to him. I wouldn't want to harm anyone though. I am just going to leave them there for the rest of their lives, or a good 5 years, and after that, I'll turn them in. The way I know that you know Braden Park is that I have spy cameras in my bunker. Funny coincidence right, well, it isn't. Your great-grandmother owns the land right. Well, she is my grandmother, and I found out from my father that she has land here. He cannot keep a simple secret.

I'm your maternal uncle Denver. Has Mom ever said anything about me? Do you remember me?" The man said, which was a lot of information to take in all at once.

   "Yes, Mom has told me about you, and I remember you. The last time I saw you was... a while ago, can't remember it." I spoke. Once I had finished saying this, The Author came to the place. "So, have you made sure that all these people didn't do any of these crimes by mistake? Or maybe they did it with a cause," I said. "No, I am one hundred percent sure that they are all guilty of committing murder," he said, quite confidently. "What did Richard's mother do?" I asked. "Murdered and buried 3 people," he said. "What? Could you repeat that like... 6 times?" Richard said, shocked that his mom was a murderer. "She murdered and buried 3 people. She murdered and buried 3 people. She murdered and buried 3 people. She murdered and buried 3 people. She murdered and buried 3 people. She murdered and buried 3 people." He said, quite quickly.

"I didn't mean literally." He said. Now both of us were extremely scared. I took this as an opportunity to release the anesthesia. I pressed a button, and he realized that he was drugged and said, "Denver, you dirty..." and fell on the sidewalk, unconscious. I lifted him and put him in his SUV. I then took Richard's mom out and I thought. Was it possible that I have been helping a murderer this whole time? She was still unconscious from the chloroform. My uncle should be out for a good amount of time. I used the time machine and transported him into the bunker and locked it. He will wake up in the bunker. Now I must take the duty of interrogating the people, which has not been done by my uncle. So, The Author, Richard, and I went to the bunker, and we carried Richard's mother into the time machine and went to the second that we left to come here to let Richard's mother to be kidnapped. We were back. Now I had to interrogate around 25 people, 26 if you include Richard's mother. Like I've said before, interrogation is hard. 26 people, what they say to me in these few minutes will change their lives forever.

Chapter 35

So I interrogated every person besides Richard's mom, who was still drugged. I found out that 14 of the people killed or caused death with cause. I let them stay in our bunker. The rest of the people stayed in their bunker, and I locked them in there, where they would stay for another 5 years, or until they die. The other people will be released. I'm also not going to do anything about my uncle. He did all this for a good cause; to eliminate bad people from the world. I left my uncle a note. This is what it had on it:

Dear Uncle,

All the people in the bunker with you are innocent. Please let them go. The ones in your bunker are not innocent, so punish them as you wish. Forgive me, and do not tell my past self that this occurred.

The key to your bunker is under the big rock by the tall tree.

D.C.

He may kill them, or he may just turn them in after 5 years. Nobody knows. Not even The Author. Nobody knows the fate of the people who are in the other bunker. Nobody knows.

I had a knife. I brought a knife here. Finally, Mrs. James woke up. Nobody was around. I put the knife to her neck, it was my first time threatening someone. I started talking. "Tell me the truth and nothing happens to either of us. Don't make me use the knife. I will only use it if you do not cooperate. Now, is it true that you killed 3 people?" I asked.

"Yes, they came to my house and tried robbing it. I killed them all brutally, and I was afraid that I would get in trouble, because I did not kill them for self-defense. I used some general anesthesia and made them faint, and after that I tied them up and cut them up in ways that nobody can imagine. I made them suffer and I feel no remorse. None. I had a gun, and I could have used it, but no, I cut them up, burned them, and threw their remains into Lower Derby Lake, you know, that lake in the northeast part of our city. I killed them, yes, but with a good reason. They broke into my house to take stuff, so I took their lives in the most brutal way possible." she said, without any emotion. My knife was foldable, so I folded it and put it in my pocket. Richard's mom got up.

"Forget any of this happened. I was scared that I was helping a murderer. Turns out that you did it with a cause. I would've done the same." I told her this, and she smiled.

"Now you have to live in the bunker for two years," I said. I called Richard, who came in a while. He was just walking with The Author, and talking, and had no clue that I threatened his mom.

A while later...

I washed my temporary hair dye off. My uncle released all the people that were innocent, and he wasn't caught. Richard and I both made his mother stay in the bunker for two years. We gave her food and whatever she needed using the time machine. My uncle forgave me. I had saved the lives of 15 innocent people. My job was done. My life had a purpose. It finally had a purpose.

The reunion was nice. Nobody suspected anything. Once Richard's mother came back, we burned the bunkers down. Nobody found anything. We were safe. No more stalkers, no more kidnappers, at least, none that will interfere in our lives now. Richard's father gave me a couple thousand dollars. We paid off our bank loan using some art that Richard's mom made. We made a good profit out of it too, but I gave it all to Richard's mom when she "came back from the dead."

Everything is good.

Chapter 36

The Author showed up behind me and smiled at me.

"I appreciate what you did, but I have one thing to tell you."

"What?" I asked.

"To make money, you shouldn't go into the past and change it. It's too risky. You might change something you don't want to. You should go into the future," he said.

"Okay, I will." I told him. Then he gave me a note.

This is what it had:

"Rewind and change history, or fast forward and sell the future!"

That was exactly what I was going to do.

My story hasn't ended.

It had just begun.

Acknowledgments

I would like to thank anyone who supported me through my journey of writing. I would also like to thank my 5th grade teacher, and my classmate, who got me into writing. The story goes like this: My classmate wrote something and told everyone the story, and in jealousy, I wrote one too, and found out that I liked writing.

I would like to thank any of my ELA and math teachers who taught me, and the other teachers as well. I would like to thank my parents for supporting me. Last but not least, I would like to thank anyone who has read this book and has read this acknowledgements section, because you wouldn't be reading this if you haven't. It's an endless loop my friend discovered.

This is my first novel, written at the age of 13, and published at the age of 14.

Thanks,

Abdur Rahman

www.ingramcontent.com/pod-product-compliance
Lightning Source LLC
Chambersburg PA
CBHW070750120626
46557CB00002B/532